Snowman Paul Saves Kate's Birthday

Written by Yossi Lapid
Illustrated by Joanna Pasek

ISBN 978-0-9973899-4-4

I dedicate this book to the beloved memory
of my three parents: Ilona Farkas,
Shmuel Farkas and Magda Farkas.

Kate's party was set for tomorrow
And there were all these rules to follow.

**But then, I made a big mistake —
When — oops! —**

"Paul," I said, "I'm very sad.
I think I messed up really bad!"

"It happened — *poof!* — out of the blue.
Somehow, entirely by mistake,
I ate my sister's birthday cake."

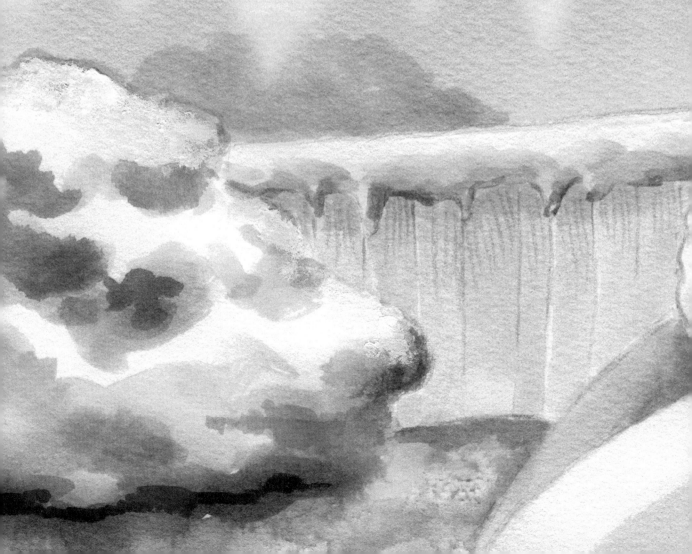

"Oh, wow!" gasped Paul,

"A HUGE MISTAKE!

But there's a way to set things right
If you and I work hard tonight."

"Really?" I asked. "Tell me your plan,
And I'll do everything I can!"

We worked all night, in bright moonlight,
And in the morning, what a sight!

We built a wonderland for Kate
To help her laugh and celebrate.

When Kate awoke and saw the sight
She jumped and squealed in great delight.

A merry-go-round made of snow,

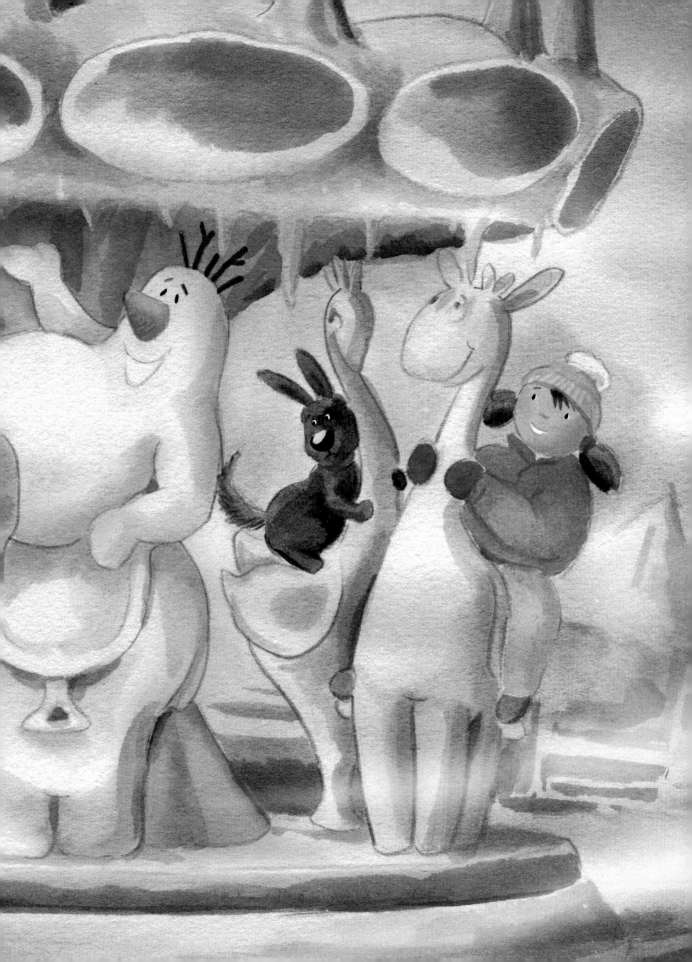

A very special puppet show,

A giant seesaw made of ice,

A royal carriage pulled by mice.

We played,
We laughed,
We had great fun,
Under the friendly winter sun.

Then Kate said, "Now, we need a break –
Let's go and eat my birthday cake!"

"Wait Kate!" I said. "Let's play some more.
We have this magic candy store,
And you can have a magic shake..."

"No way," she said. "I want MY cake!"

We froze in place. What would Kate say
When she looked at that empty tray?

And as for Mom, I had no clue
What she was now going to do.

**But then, as we approached the door
There was a nice surprise in store!**

We jumped for joy — hip hip hooray!
Mom found the way to save the day!

But then Mom said, right off the bat:
"Don't pull another trick like that!"

"Don't worry Mom, I love my sis,
I really learned a lot from this!"

Made in the USA
Columbia, SC
15 November 2018